Faint Frogs Feeling Feverish

Faint Frogs
Feeling
Feverish

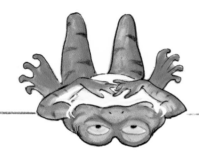

& other terrifically tantalizing
tongue twisters by

Lilian Obligado

PUFFIN BOOKS

To Tina, Sziga,
Ted, Tommy, Susie,
Sergio, and Andrés

PUFFIN BOOKS
Viking Penguin Inc., 40 West 23rd Street, New York, New York 10010, U.S.A.
Penguin Books Ltd, Harmondsworth, Middlesex, England
Penguin Books Australia Ltd, Ringwood, Victoria, Australia
Penguin Books Canada Limited, 2801 John Street, Markham, Ontario, Canada L3R 1B4
Penguin Books (N.Z.) Ltd, 182–190 Wairau Road, Auckland 10, New Zealand

First published by Viking Penguin Inc. 1983
Published in Picture Puffins 1986

Library of Congress Cataloging in Publication Data
Obligado, Lilian.   Faint frogs feeling feverish.
Summary: An alphabet book featuring names of animals used in
alliterative phrases describing unusual activities.
    1. English language—Alphabet—Juvenile literature.
2. Tongue twisters—Juvenile literature.   [1. Alphabet.
2. Tongue twisters.   3. Animals—Pictorial works]
I. Title.
PE1155.018   1986   [E]   84-18117   ISBN 0-14-050507-5

Printed in Japan
by Dai Nippon

A Aardvark adding

Antelope attending
ailing Alpaca

Auk arresting Ape

and Armadillo
ably assisting

Anteater admiring Ant

Boar boldly bathing

Beavers building
beautiful boat

Biscuit-bearing Beetles
bringing beer, berries, bread

C

Crab carefully
crowning Crow

Cheerfully chattering Chipmunks choosing chocolate chip cookies

Cat cooking Codfish

D

Deer driving
dangerously

E

Elephant eagerly eating Easter eggs

F

Friendly Fox
fixing faucet

Ferrets fencing

Flamingo fanning
faint Frog
feeling feverish

G

Gorilla greeting galloping Giraffe

Goats getting goggles

Hamsters hurrying home

I

Iguana inviting Ibis, ignoring Inchworm

Jaguars jogging

Jackrabbit juggling

J

Jerboa joyfully jumping

L

Lions loving

Lizard looking lonely

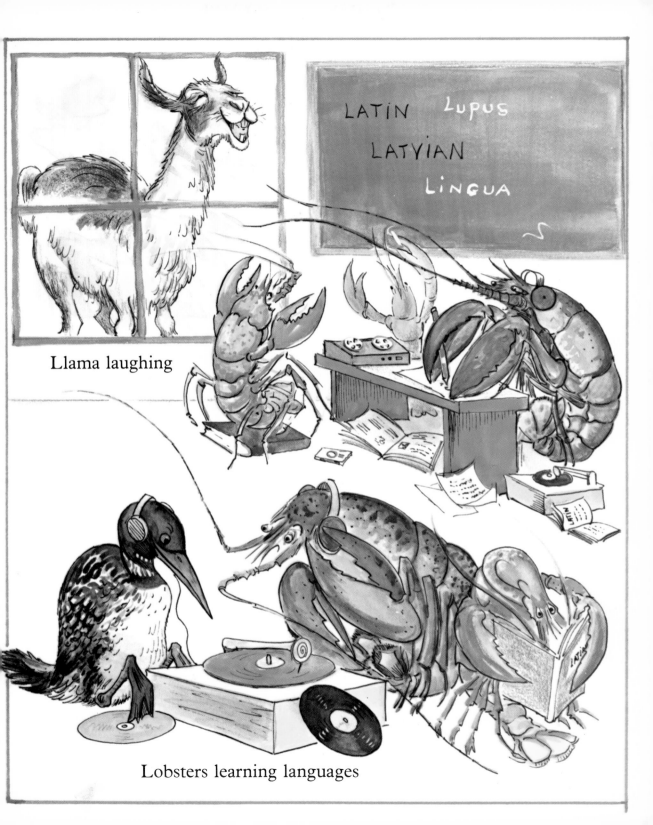

Llama laughing

Lobsters learning languages

M

Monkey measuring Moose

Macaw meeting Mallard

Messy Mice making marmalade

Mr. Mongoose marrying Miss Mole

N

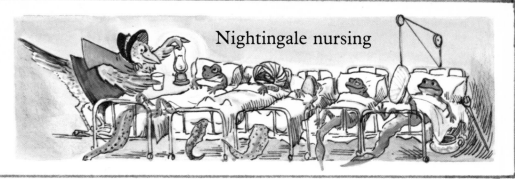

Nightingale nursing

O

Octopus opening Oysters

Overweight Otter ordering olives

Owl observing

P

Patrolling Panda pursuing Panther
pickpockets packing purple pistols

Penguins paying Pangolin

Platypus
painting
portraits

Quails quietly quilting

R

Robin relaxing

Rhinoceros
racing Roadrunner

Rich Rabbits resting, reading rave reviews

S

Smiling Snakes sipping
strawberry sodas

Sole soulfully sighing

Shy Spider spinning

Squinting Squid seeing
ship slowly sinking

Swordfish sawing

Seal selling seashells

Two Toucans
tying ties

Turtles tasting tea

Traveling Turkeys taking train

Tigers trying trousers

Toad telling timid Termite tall tale

U

Urial using ugly umbrella

Uakari undoing untidy undershirt

Voles voting

W

Wealthy Walrus wearing waistcoat, washing Wallaby

Woodchucks watering
woodland wildflowers

Wolf whistling, waking Wombat

X

Xemo X-raying Xiphias

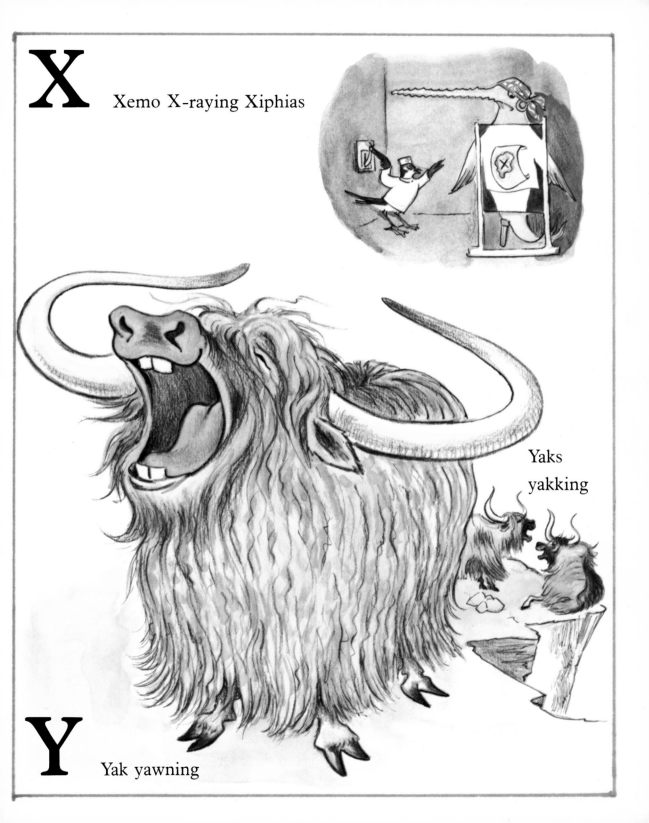

Y

Yaks
yakking

Yak yawning

Z

Zebra zipping zipper